# animals WHY?

## WHY DO BUNNIES HOP?

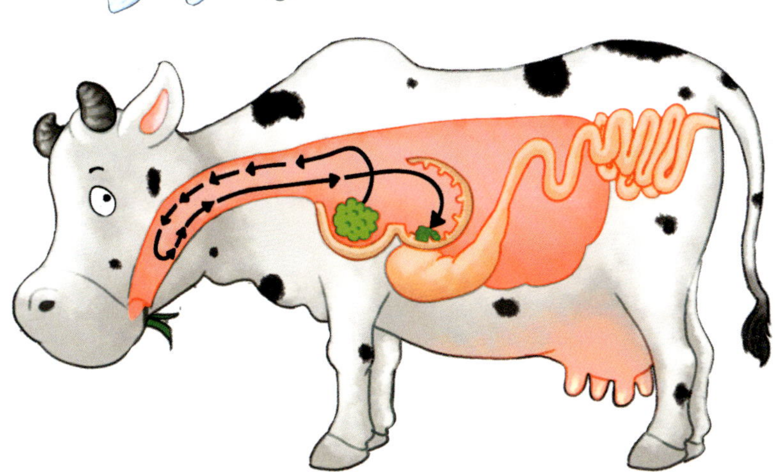

Om KIDZ
An imprint of Om Books International

# WHY?

## CONTENTS

WHY?

**Find out!**

How far can honeybees fly in an hour?

## 1 Why do honeybees die after they sting?

Because they leave behind their stingers! Honeybees usually sting when they find their hive in danger. The stinger of a honeybee is made of two barbed lancets. When the bee stings, it is unable to pull out the stinger. The stinger is left with a part of the bee's digestive tract, muscles and nerves. This is why bees die after stinging someone.

## 2 Why is a praying mantis called so?

**Pocket fact**

A praying mantis has only one ear, located on the bottom of its abdomen. The ear is specially developed to detect the echolocation calls of a bat, but can't hear other sounds too well!

Because of its legs! A praying mantis is a part of the hemimetabola group of insects. These insects do not undergo a complete metamorphosis and live in both hot and moderate climatic conditions. The front legs of a praying mantis are bent and held at an angle that makes it look like it is praying. This peculiar posture gives the praying mantis its name.

## Find out!

What is the weight of an adult female mosquito?

## 3 Why does a monarch butterfly feed on milkweed in its larval stage?

They help it turn into a beautiful butterfly and more! The larva of a monarch butterfly feeds only on milkweed because it allows the larva to grow and keep all the vitamins needed to transform into a beautiful butterfly. Also, while eating these weeds, the larva stores a poison called cardiac glycosides from milkweed leaves. This toxin helps defend itself from enemies such as lizards, birds, and frogs.

## 4 Why do only female mosquitoes bite?

Blood is their source of protein! A female mosquito cannot lay eggs if it does not have a protein source. When a female mosquito sits on you, it sticks its long, thin proboscis into your skin like a sharp pin. It then injects a fluid inside your skin which keeps your blood from thickening. Then it sucks some blood and stores it in its abdomen and flies away to lay her eggs.

### Pocket fact

The monarch butterfly migrates from Canada to Mexico in winters. It uses the Earth's magnetic field and the position of the Sun to find its way to Mexico, and spends the winter there to avoid the cold weather.

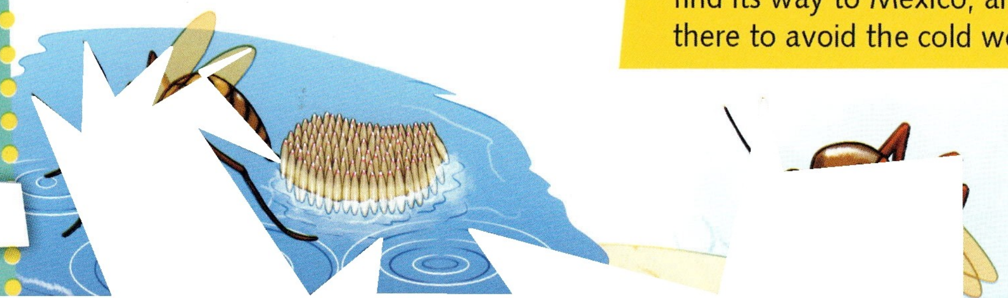

**WHY?**

**Find out!**

Which predator is not affected by a skunk's stink?

## 5 Why do skunks stink?

To keep predators away! Skunks stink only when they need to keep their enemies away. When a skunk feels threatened, it releases a special spray from glands underneath its tail. The spray is made of oily chemicals called thiols that are sulphur compounds. This makes the skunk stink and keeps its predators, such as wolves, foxes and badgers, away.

**Pocket fact**

The Alpine Marmot is the largest squirrel species. It can grow up to a whooping 73 centimetres!

## 6 Why do squirrels have a bushy tail?

For balance and more! A squirrel uses its tail to keep steady as it leaps across trees. It also uses the tail to communicate with other squirrels. When a squirrel is alarmed, it flicks its tail, and when it is aggressive, it fluffs it up. By wrapping the tail around themselves, squirrels stay warm during the cold months of winter, and also use the tail as a sunshade to protect themselves from the sun during summer!

## Find out!

How many teeth does an alligator have?

# 7 Why do snakes shed their skin?

So they can grow! Snakes replace their old skin with a new one to allow growth and to remove parasites from their skin. The skin of a snake stretches and wears out as it grows. The growth stops after a few months and a new skin, with the same pattern and colour as the old one, grows underneath. When the new skin grows completely, the old skin is shed along with parasites, if any.

## Pocket fact

The Titanoboa snake lived 60 million years ago and is the longest, largest and heaviest snake that has ever been discovered.

# 8 Why do alligators seem so lazy?

Because they spend a lot of time doing nothing! By doing nothing, alligators control their body temperature. Alligators are cold-blooded animals, i.e., their body temperature changes with the changing environmental temperature. They often lie in the sun to warm themselves up. To keep itself cool, an alligator lies with its mouth open—to let heat escape from its body.

**Find out!**

Unscramble the letters to find what we call a young female cow who has not given birth? RHFEIE

# 9 Why does red colour make bulls charge?

The red colour has no effect on the bulls at all! In fact, bulls, like all other cattle, are colour-blind. What irritates them is the waving of cloth. If you vigorously wave a cloth in front of a bull, it gets irritated and this makes it charge, not the colour of the cloth.

**Pocket fact**

The world record for the heaviest bull goes to a Chianina. It is an Italian breed of cattle, named Donetto. It weighs 1,740 kilograms! Isn't it amazing?

# 10 Why does a cow keep chewing its food?

Because it doesn't chew it in the first go! A cow eats the food quickly, and chews just a little to moisten it and then swallows. The food goes into the first section of its stomach—the rumen, mixes with digestive liquids and is softened. This softened food is called cud. Next, the cud is sent back to the cow's mouth where it is re-chewed and swallowed again, so that it can go to other parts of the stomach and get digested.

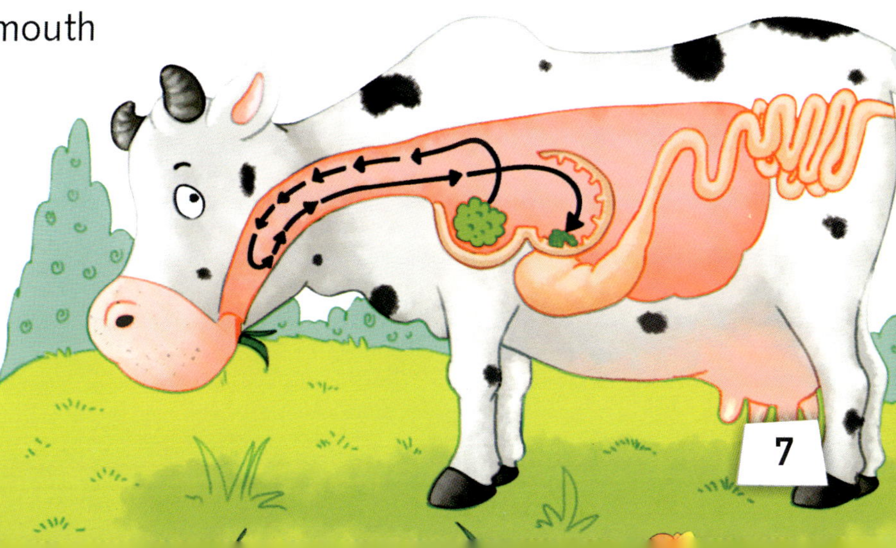

## Find out!

What is special about a rabbit's eyes?

# 11 Why do rats bite on things so much?

To wear out their teeth! Rats have four long, sharp front teeth called incisors (two on the top and two on the bottom). These incisors have a special shape for gnawing. They are open-rooted which means they never stop growing. So, rats keep biting things constantly to wear their teeth down. If they don't do so, their incisors would grow at an 86° angle in a spiral, that would make it impossible for the rat to eat or even close its mouth!

## Pocket fact

Safe landing!
Rats are somewhat similar to their enemy-cats. A rat can fall from a height of 50 feet and land safely!

# 12 Why do bunnies hop?

Because their legs are of different length! A bunny's legs are quite different from yours: their front legs are shorter and the back legs are long and strong. Due to this difference in the length, with a single push of the back legs, they leap high in the forward direction and land on their front legs. This movement is called hopping. Hopping also helps them balance, while their back legs spring forward and get ready for another leap!

**Find out!**

How many hearts does an octopus have?

# 13 Why is an octopus's blood blue?

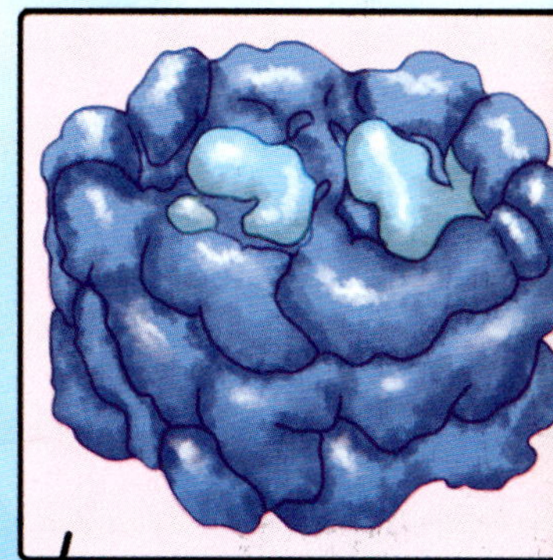

Hemocyanin gives it the blue colour! The blood of an octopus is blue due to a pigment called hemocyanin, a blood-borne protein with copper atoms that bind with oxygen atoms giving the blue colour. The pigment allows the octopus to get a constant oxygen supply, even when it isn't readily available in the environment. This helps them survive even at a temperature of -1.8° Celsius!

# 14 Why do sea anemones wait for their prey to swim by?

A sea anemone has a sticky foot called a basal disc. The foot of the anemone is attached to the surface that it lies on. Sea anemones spend most of their time attached to rocks at the bottom of the sea or on coral reefs. So in order to eat, they wait for their food (fish, shrimp, etc.) to swim by. They sting with their tentacles, and then push them into their mouth.

**Pocket fact**

Octopus wrestling was a popular sport in the 1960s. In this sport, a diver had to find an octopus in shallow water and drag it to the surface!

**Find out!**

Lion is the national symbol of which country?

# 15 Why do lions have loose belly skin?

For their own protection! Lions make several adaptations in order to fit into their habitat. Some of these are loose belly skin, a thick mane, heavy shoulders and forelimbs. While heavy limbs help them pin down prey, the loose belly skin protects them during fights. The loose belly skin ensures that the lion is not severely injured if attacked by the prey.

**Pocket fact**

Siberian tigers are known to be the heaviest of the subspecies of tigers, weighing around 225 kilograms. The lightest subspecie is the Sumatran, weighing about 90 kilograms.

# 16 Why do tigers have sharp projections on their tongue?

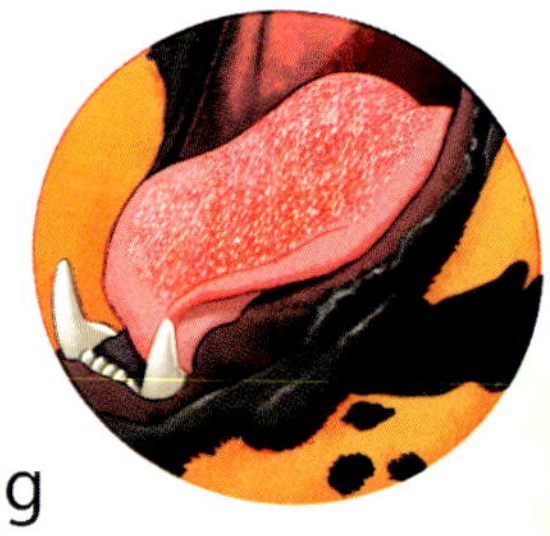

To help them tear into their food! A tiger's tongue is covered with numerous papillae. These are small, sharp, and rearfacing projections. The papillae give the tongue a rough texture, that helps the tiger strip feathers, fur and meat from its prey's body.

**Find out!**

What is a group of jellyfish called?

## 17 Why are jellyfish named so?

Jellyfish are not fish.They belong to a class of creatures called scyphozoa. The body of a jellyfish is made up of a jellylike substance called mesoglea. This jelly has a one-cell thick layer of skin around it. This is what gives jellyfish its name. Interestingly, the body of a jellyfish is mostly made up of water, around 90 per cent!

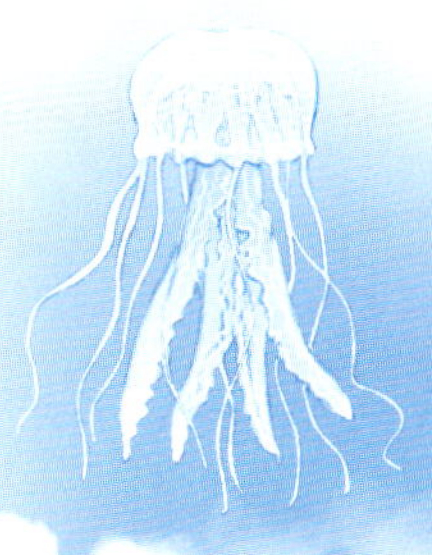

**Pocket fact**

Goldfish don't have a stomach. This is why they are fed easily digestible food in small feeding sessions.

## 18 Why do fish have scales?

To protect them! All fish, except the catfish and the lamprey, have scales. Scales are bony in structure; they overlap each other to protect the body of the fish. The scales can easily bend and slide over one another. This helps the fish move from side to side and swim.

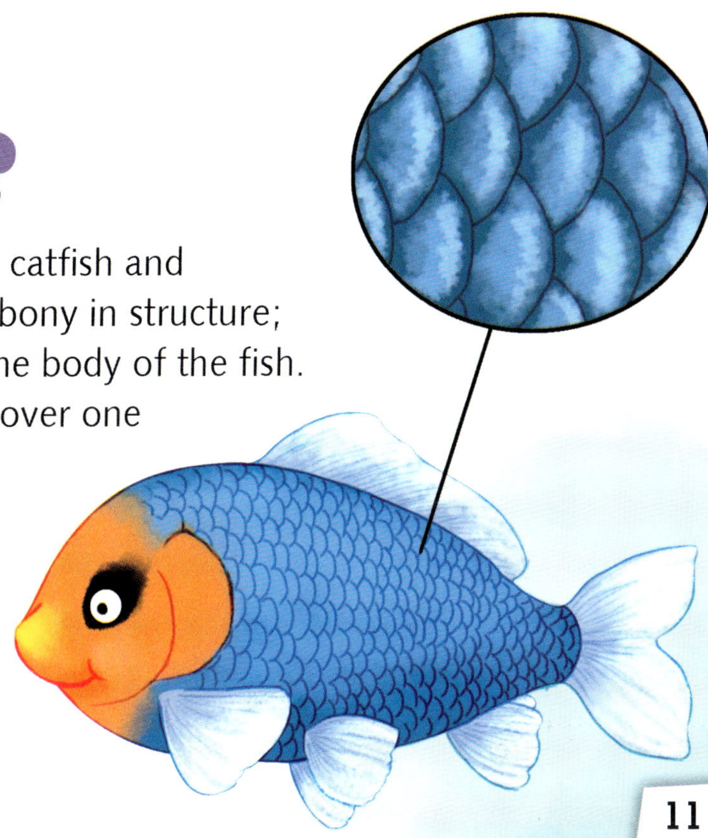

## Find out!

Which is the largest parrot? What is different about this parrot?

# 19 Why do humming birds eat so much?

Because they fly a lot! A hummingbird is a very small bird with poorly developed feet that can barely walk. So it flies a lot and a great deal of its energy is spent in flying. It also has a high metabolism, i.e., it consumes calories quickly. So it must eat regularly to gain high energy to keep flying.

## Pocket fact

Hummingbirds are migratory birds. The rufous hummingbird has the longest migration period of the species. It travels a distance of more than 3,000 miles from its nesting grounds in Alaska and Canada to its winter habitat in Mexico.

# 20 Why are parrots different from other birds?

Because of their beak and feet! A parrot's beak is hinged (both upper and lower). It can raise the upper part of its beak without moving the whole head! Parrots are the only birds that can use their feet to lift up food to their mouths. Also, no other group of birds have a range of colours similar to parrots.

**Find out!**

What gave the bald eagle its name?

## 21 Why does an eagle have a hole in its tongue?

To help it breathe! The windpipe of an eagle comes through a hole on the tongue, to help it breathe. The tongue also has a sort of barb on it. This barb helps it pull food into its throat, where it is then swallowed. While the eagle extends its tongue to allow the barb to grab the food, the hole in the tongue opens and the eagle can take a breath of fresh air!

**Pocket fact**

Woodpeckers can peck up to 20 times per second, a total of 8,000-12,000 pecks per day! They do this for feeding, excavating nest cavities and drumming.

## 22 Why do woodpeckers have tiny feathers over their nostrils?

The feathers protect the nose! Woodpeckers are interesting birds with distinctive long beaks. A woodpecker uses its beak to make holes in trees and dig out small insects living under the bark to feed on. The tiny bristle-like feathers over their nostrils help keep wood particles from being inhaled.

**Find out!**

What is the difference between a deer and a reindeer?

# 23 Why do a reindeer's hooves change with seasons?

To help them walk! Reindeers live in tundra (very cold) regions. These cover Northern Asia, Europe, Siberia, Alaska, North America, Canada and Greenland. Their hooves adapt to changing seasons. In summer, tundra regions become wet and damp, so the reindeers' footpads become sponge-like. This gives them a bigger surface area to walk on the wet ground. In winter, when there is snow around, their footpads shrink and tighten to avoid slipping.

**Pocket fact**

The largest and the smallest!
The largest breed of hamster is the Cricetus cricetus. It is an European breed and can measure up to 13.4 inches long. On the other hand, the smallest hamster is the genus Phodopus, only two to four inches long!

# 24 Why do hamsters have large cheek pouches?

To store food! Hamsters are small rodents that originally belong to East Asia. They eat nuts, seeds, vegetables, grass, fruits and berries. When a hamster finds food, it stores it in its large cheek pouches. It then stores the food in underground burrows for future use!

**Find out!**

Have you heard about a pygmy hippo? How is it different from a regular hippo?

# 25 Why does a hippo 'sweat blood'?

They don't sweat blood at all! Hippo is a large animal with thick skin, especially over its back and rump. Its body is almost hairless, so it has neither sweat nor sebaceous glands to produce sweat. But hippos have unique glands that produce a thick red fluid. This fluid helps its skin from drying and cracking when it is out of water. This leads to the myth that hippos 'sweat blood'.

**Pocket fact**

Proboscis monkeys eat fruits that are unripe. This is because the sugars in ripe fruits can ferment in their stomach and cause fatal bloating.

# 26 Why is the nose of a proboscis monkey special?

The male's nose can grow very big! A proboscis monkey is a species of monkeys in which the males have long noses. In fact, its nose can grow so big that it hangs over its mouth! It is believed that proboscis monkeys have long noses to attract female monkeys. They make the monkey's sound echo louder, impressing the females in the area!

# OTHER TITLES IN THIS SERIES

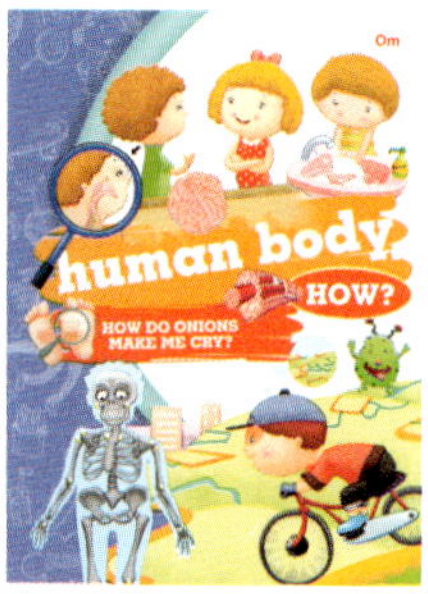

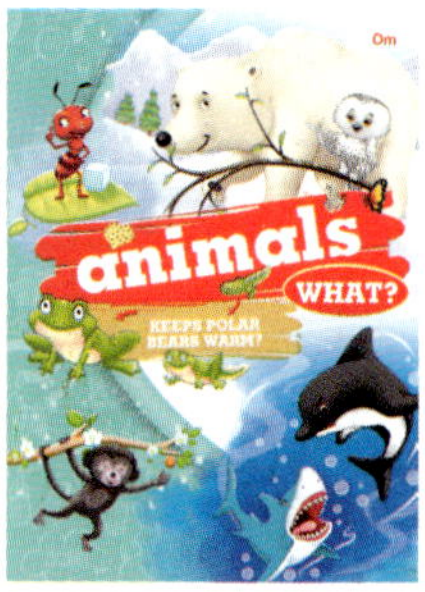

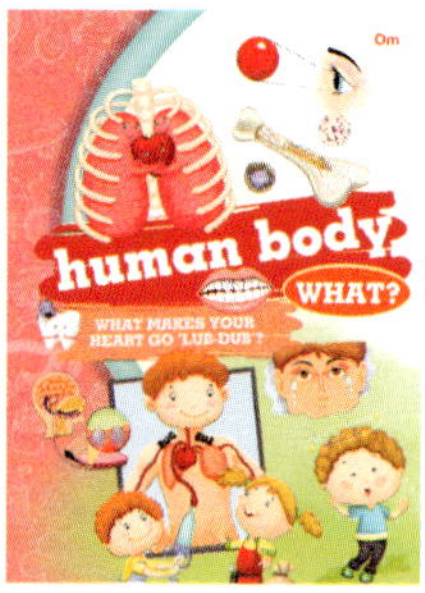


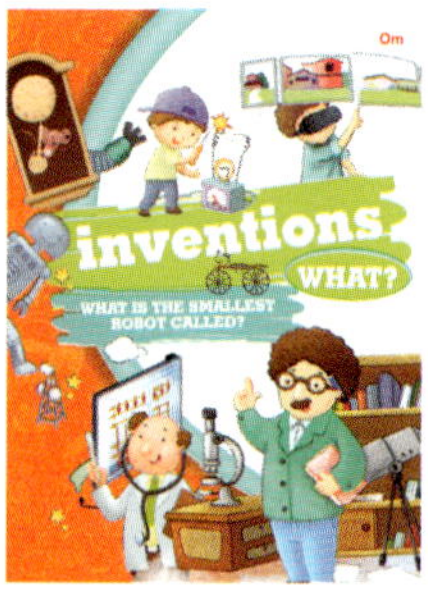

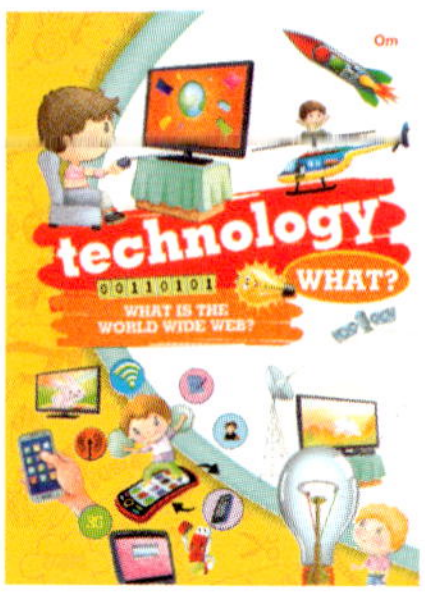

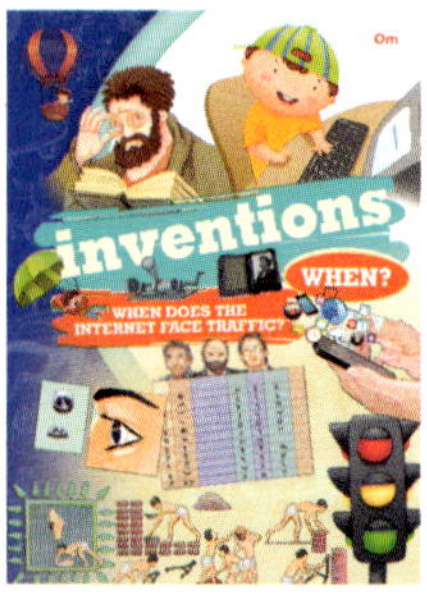

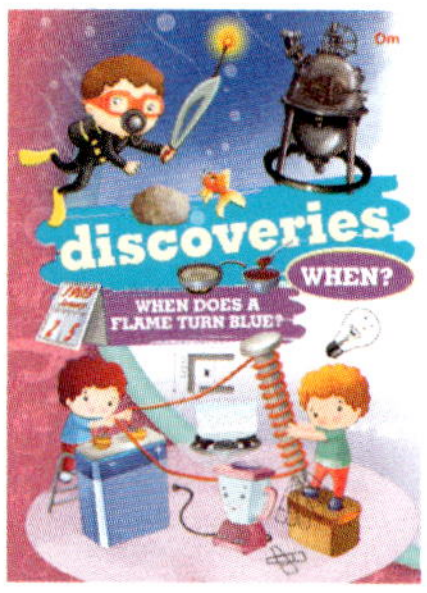

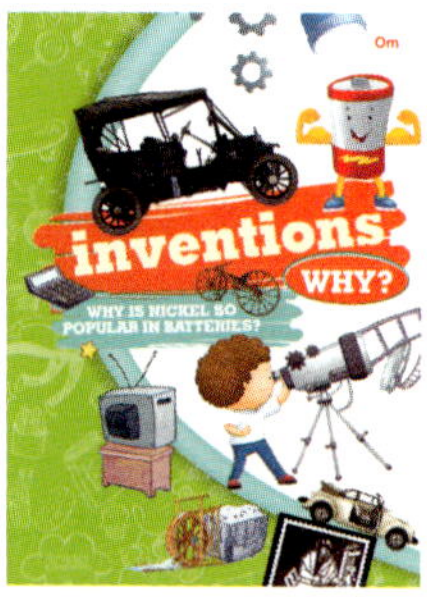

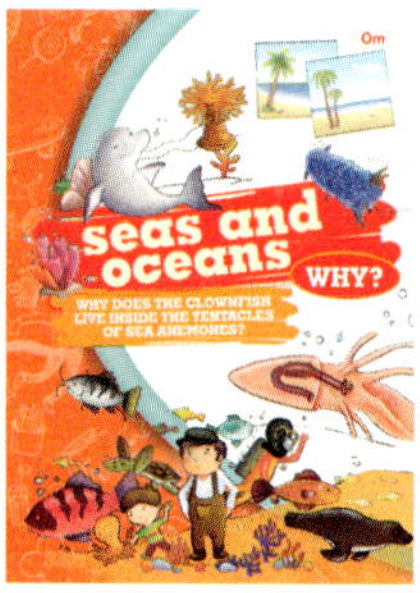

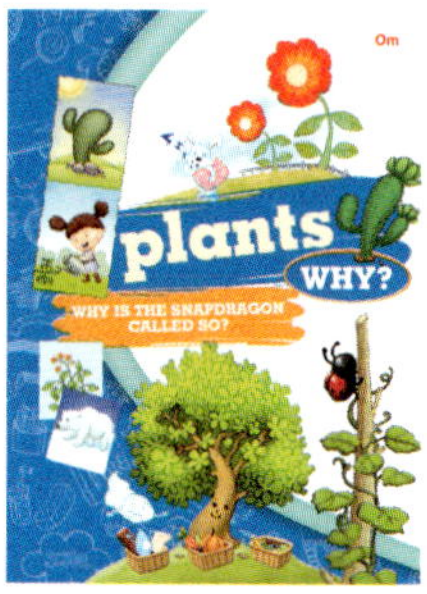